Ocoee & Other Stories

WINNERS OF THE COMMONWEALTH
SHORT STORY PRIZE 2023

PAPER
+ INK

Ocoee & Other Stories:

Winners of the Commonwealth Short Story Prize 2023

This edition has been published in 2023
in the United Kingdom by Paper + Ink.

**PAPER
+ INK**

www.paperand.ink
Twitter: @paper_andink
Instagram: paper_and.ink

"Ocoee" © Kwame McPherson
"The Undertaker's Apprentice" © Hana Gammon
"Oceans Away from My Homeland" © Agnes Chew
"Lech, Prince and the Nice Things" © Rue Baldry
"Kilinochchi" © Himali McInnes

1 2 3 4 5 6 7 8 9 10

ISBN 9781911475668

A CIP catalogue record for this book is available from the British Library.
Jacket design by James Nunn: www.jamesnunn.co.uk | @Gnunkse
Printed and bound in Great Britain.

Commonwealth
Foundation

COMMONWEALTH
SHORT STORY PRIZE

CONTENTS

CONTENTS

ABOUT THE COMMONWEALTH SHORT STORY PRIZE

The Commonwealth Short Story Prize is administered by the Commonwealth Foundation. Now in its twelfth year, the prize is awarded for the best piece of unpublished short fiction (2,000 – 5,000 words). Regional winners receive GBP 2,500, and the overall winner receives GBP 5,000. It is free to enter and open to citizens of all the countries of the Commonwealth. Entries can be submitted in Bengali, Chinese, English, French, Greek, Malay, Portuguese, Samoan, Swahili, Tamil and Turkish, as well as the Creole languages of the Commonwealth. They can also be translated into English from any language. The international panel of judges selects one winner from each of the five Commonwealth regions – Africa; Asia; Canada

and Europe; the Caribbean; and the Pacific – one of whom is chosen as the overall winner.

CSSP 2023 Judging Panel

Chair: Bilal Tanweer
Africa: Rémy Ngamije
Asia: Ameena Hussein
Canada and Europe: Katrina Best
Caribbean: Mac Donald Dixon
Pacific: Dr Selina Tusitala Marsh

About the Commonwealth Foundation

The Commonwealth Foundation is an intergovernmental organisation established by heads of government in support of the belief that the Commonwealth is as much an association of peoples as it is of governments. It is the Commonwealth agency for civil society; an organisation dedicated to strengthening people's participation in all aspects of public dialogue, so they can act together and learn from

each other to build free, open, and democratic societies. Its cultural programming is founded on the belief that well-told stories can help people make sense of events and take action to bring about change. The Foundation works with local and international partners to identify and deliver a wide range of cultural projects and platforms, including *adda*, an online magazine of new writing.

www.commonwealthfoundation.com
www.addastories.org

OCOEE

KWAME MCPHERSON

I was indecisive about whether to halt or whether I had enough gas, junk food and music. On my car's player, Michael Jackson was singing about "Ben". I had liked that movie as a kid, and loved the Jacksons even more. Still, I needed to have a rest, use a washroom and stretch my legs. The sun was going down, and I would've been miles ahead of where I was if it hadn't been for the delay. One tire puncture was easier to deal with than two: a headache I did not need, but one I had to deal with nonetheless, taking hours rather than minutes from my schedule. To say I was peeved would be an understatement.

I made up my mind that the next town would be the place I laid my head for the night. Especially with that creeping tiredness touching my eyes, which drooped a few times with the

intention to close. I fought against it as best I could. I wanted some hot food. The last time I had eaten properly was five hours earlier, and junk food was not healthy at the best of times.

A large moon shone like a massive spotlight, illuminating a barren landscape undulating as far as my eyes could see, dark fissures highlighted by the bright white light. Further to my right, and miles away, a dark, rugged line seemed to follow me – a continuous ragged mountain range. Its name escaped me. To my left was nothing but complete emptiness, and that up-and-down land.

Michael was now living "life off the wall", and my fingers tapped the beat on the steering wheel. I always enjoyed him, my favourite artist in the whole world. Glancing at my GPS, I couldn't see any town for miles around. I imagined that, if there was one, it'd be like the many I had already passed: small, with strip malls on both sides of the highway and a café, a greasy eatery for truckers and short-stay passers-through, a gas station, pharmacy and the inevitable sheriff's station. The school or hospital would be miles away and not easily seen from the highway.

Suddenly, a *ping*. I glanced at the notification; a blob that had not been there before appeared on my GPS. The name of the place was "Ocoee". I squinted. There *was* a town up ahead; I could see lights on the horizon, and the outlines of buildings. Its name made no impression on me; it sounded like one those haunted places always found in the back of some beyond. I snickered at my own joke. I was not that way inclined, to be afraid of the dark, and I had only heard about that stuff growing up in the Caribbean: Grandpops told us young ones about Rolling Calf, the Lonely Woman and Black H'art Man. His stories freaked out my sister and brother, but I was always cool. Now an ex-army man, and seeing all that I have seen on my tours, I was certain I would not be scared of any haunted place or people. But I was only fooling myself. There were many nights when sleep was hard to come. I laughed even louder, listening to Michael face a "thriller night".

I must have been less than a mile from the town when blinking blue and red lights suddenly flashed in my rear-view. I had not seen

them creep up on me, and must have missed the cruiser's headlights. Maybe I was just lost with Michael in "The Lady in My Life" – well, in *his* life. My lady was nowhere 'round. I had learned from experience never to stop on lonely, dark roads. One night in the city, against years of knowing and my better judgment, I had stopped for a cop car that had trailed me for over five blocks. They said it was a regular stop, and demanded my ID – which I refused to give. Instead, I held onto my work ID and shoved it into their faces, because I knew my constitutional rights. They threatened me with arrest; according to them, I was obstructing an investigation – someone fitting my description had robbed a liquor store and was seen running away. Bear in mind I was walking home that time, had my work ID slung from a lanyard around my neck and was also carrying a heavy rucksack on my back. Nevertheless, one of the officers decided he was going to handcuff me.

I never saw the inside of their cruiser. Let's just say they came off worse, and I got off from having a police record or even seeing the inside

of a jail. My ancestors definitely were with me then, through a superb lawyer.

The headlamps and strobe lights flooded my rear-view. I kept on at a reasonable pace, not speeding, willing my rental car to reach the town's streetlights. I was just on the outskirts of Ocoee when the cruiser sped up, overtook me and skidded to a stop just in front of my car, blocking my way. I screeched to a halt.

I waited to be approached by the cop or cops, but nobody came from the cruiser. I had glanced at my dashboard clock just as I'd slammed on the brakes, and now saw that five minutes had elapsed. I wondered what they were waiting for. Trying to make me sweat? Running my vehicle's plate? I gave it another two minutes. Finally, I watched both doors slowly open, and two state troopers alight.

They walked over confidently, one officer tall and thin and the other short and fat. Tweedledee and Tweedledum. I chuckled. With their flashlights blinding me, and about a metre from my front windows, the taller one stood back and shouted: "Let me see your hands!"

I stuck them out my window. The fat one worked his way to the passenger side, brilliant light brightening my car's interior.

"Where you headed, boy?" *"Boy"*? I thought. *Is this not 2023?*

"Do you need to see my driver's licence and documents?" I asked. I was not about to call him *sir*, or rise to the bait.

"I asked you a question, boy." *"Boy", again.*

"Do you need to see my papers?" I demanded.

"I do the telling here, boy." *Third time.*

I said nothing, my hands still out the window. I knew how these traffic stops frequently went, and I could already see tomorrow's news headlines. That is, if anyone ever even heard about my passing – or should I say *killing*. I was in the boonies, nowhere in particular. No other vehicle around, nothing but a wide expanse of empty land and a town away in the distance. I was alone and isolated. But I was not scared. During the last Gulf War, there was an incident in which my unit and I became separated in the Iraqi desert. I happened on an Iraqi patrol. After a brief firefight, I needed to evade capture,

which meant being stealthy and doing grotesque
stuff to careless stragglers. I had seen too much
on my tour, death a constant companion. I had
been scared *then*.

"Get out. NOW!"

"Can I have your name and badge number?"

He did not answer. Instead, he pointed the light
into the back seat, as if looking for something.
I could see him better with the deflected light
and noticed his hand on his sidearm. I was not
about to comply. I had seen too many incidences
of Black men stepping out of their vehicles and
dying. A friend of mine ended up that way. It
was heartbreaking, attending his funeral and
watching his family, especially his mother,
wailing in complete sorrow. I wanted to kill
those cops who had killed him.

"Boy, you heard me?" *Fourth.*

There would not be a fifth time calling me
boy. That's how suddenly it happened, whatever
it was. I saw the flicker of movement in my wing
mirror, far in the distance. The light rapidly
increased in size. Orangey-red, hues constantly
shifting like a '60s kaleidoscope lamp I once

saw in a thrift store. The colours reminded me of being in the field, artillery fire lighting up the sky, launching shells at an unseen enemy. The tints now looked just like the flames that flashed from the mortar spouts. I watched the orb grow.

Officer Fats saw it first and turned to look, eyes widening in terror. He mouthed rather than said: *"What the hell!"*

The bright ball swiftly consumed my mirror, and Officer Tall must have caught the light from the corner of his eye. He drew his weapon. Involuntarily, I flinched and ducked down onto the passenger seat. I wanted to make certain I gave myself a living chance.

Abruptly, I heard both officers shouting in panic; then a barrage of shots shattered the night. They emptied their clips. I counted over seventeen shots; none splintered my windows or smashed into my car. A white light blinded me. I stayed low, covering my head with my arms. Even with my eyes shut tight, I saw the hues morph in their multi-coloured dance. There was a loud *whoosh*, then total silence until night creatures slowly and quietly made their presence

known once again. I raised my head. The officers and their cruiser were gone. The place they once stood was vacant, as if they had never existed. The light was gone, too, the night as clammy as it had been all along. I was sweating.

Hastily, I alighted and examined the area where the officers had stood. The moon: my flashlight. *Nothing*. No bones, no blood. I sprinted to where the cruiser had been. *Nothing*. No debris, no remnants of a vehicle. It was unexplainable, and I hated mystery. I ran back and jumped into my car, started the ignition and squealed away, uncertain of what I had just experienced, wishing to be anywhere else than on that dark road. I reached the town in less than ten minutes. I was bathed in perspiration, and I couldn't stop shuddering.

The town was not what I had expected. It had far more buildings, and many more stores. But there was also something strange about it: no other vehicle was on the road, no truck, car, bike or bicycle. The well-lit, broad throughway and the intersections, with their functioning stoplights and roads that crisscrossed to somewhere, were

as empty as can be, Every store on both sides of the street seemed to have someone standing in front of it, waving. *Maybe the owners,* I thought. At first, I was unsure if they were waving at me, thinking they were just being neighbourly to those across the way. It was only when a smiling, waving, elderly Black woman pointed at me directly as I crawled by that I became self-conscious of everybody's stare. They were gesturing, too. The elderly woman reminded me of my grandmother. I waved back.

Stopping in front of a rowdy, brightly lit café called Joe's Homestyle Eatery, I got out and surveyed the area to confirm that I was seeing what I was seeing. It felt strange having that many eyes on me, everybody cheery and nodding as if I had won some prize. I entered Joe's. A door chime clanged above my head, and quiet suddenly descended on the throng. To my left was a long, mahogany bar with stools in front of it, all occupied by patrons gazing at me as one. They all smiled. Booths to my right were taken; the couples and groups in them stared and beamed at me. I wanted to check myself just to

make sure nothing on me looked funny, like my shirt half-in, half-out of my pants, or my zipper open. Behind the bar stood a big Black man with a pristine white apron around his massive frame. He edged me by at least three inches in height. I could hear pots and pans clash behind him to the rear. Something smelled good: *fried chicken*. My stomach grumbled.

I nodded and glanced around. The feeling returned. Then it dawned on me: there were no white people there. Not one. Not even on the drive in had I seen any; every single person so far was Black. Eventually, the patrons stopped staring, their murmurs and laughter returning as they paid attention to each other.

"Hey brother," said the big man behind the bar, pointing to a large, wood-framed black-and-white photo in the middle of a bare wall. "Welcome home."

Home? I cocked my head and laughed. The photo was grainy, but I could see the wide street and buildings. It looked like Ocoee in daylight. "Home? I'm only passing through, and need some hot food and somewhere to crash for the night."

The man grinned. "That's fine, brother. You're safe here, and a plate of fried chicken and doughy biscuits with a steaming cup of coffee is waiting for you."

I laughed. My stomach agreed. "Thank you."

A patron, a slim man, offered me a seat at the bar. He actually rose and proffered me the stool. I nodded, thanking him. I could not think when that had ever happened to me in the big city. No Black person – or any other person, for that matter – gave away their seat. Ever.

Chortling, the big man came over, and, true to his word, he held a plate of fried chicken, biscuits and a cup of steaming black coffee. I thanked him. He also carried a small soapdish, bowl and towel for me to wash and dry my hands.

"You're going to love the biscuits, especially."

"Why?" I asked, washing and drying my hands.

"They're just like how your Gran makes them," he chuckled.

I laughed and said, sarcastically: "Sure." And then bit into the biscuit.

It took my breath away; there was not one fault. This *was* her biscuit. I then sampled

the chicken. Now, whenever Granma did her chicken, it tasted so succulent I would close my eyes, savouring the flavour. I did that now. This was no replica; this *was* her cooking.

"No way!" Shaking my head, I opened my eyes. "Where am I? I *know* my Gran's not here."

The man guffawed. "Ocoee, of course. Doesn't it ring a bell?"

"No," I shrugged.

"Well, it should – but don't worry, you're safe and will always be. As soon as you've finished eating, your room's waiting."

Nodding, I ate my food and drank my coffee before the man directed a woman to show me where I would stay. She approached suddenly. I was puzzled; she felt familiar, too. She reminded me of my cousin Michelle.

Up from my stool, and about to walk away, I said, "I don't even know your name, sir."

He grinned. "That's fine. Just think of me as a guardian angel."

I nodded and laughed. I liked his candour, for sure; there was something comforting about him.

The woman was of medium height and shapely, with a welcoming oval face. She took my elbow and steered me across the street, which was as empty as before.

"How come there are no cars on the road?" I asked. "And where are all the white people?"

She regarded me with mysterious brown eyes. They danced as if she knew something I did not. I knew those questions to be right, as nothing added up for me about Ocoee. She said nothing until we stood before a large, brown double door to a three-floored brownstone building with continental windows. The lights were on like everywhere else, as though the town and its people never slept.

"This is where you'll be staying. There's an usher at the desk, and they'll welcome you and help you with everything you need to know. Have a good night." Those were the only words she uttered. I watched her return to the eatery.

I whispered: "Good night." She turned, smiling, and waved as if I'd stood beside her and whispered in her ear. I shook my head; Ocoee was definitely a strange town. I entered the building.

The lobby was lit by large, luminous chandeliers suspended by long wires from a white stucco ceiling. Imposing paintings covered the walls; they all depicted Africa in some way. I assumed as much – I recognised the scenery from my own travels across the continent. A lavender scent permeated the building. It reminded me of burning incense. Spacious lounge chairs and large flora in bulbous pots dotted the area. A bank of elevators stood to the right of a wide counter, where a slim man stood. He wore a goatee and had a bald head. There was something about the way he looked at me, with deep black eyes. It felt familiar. Another person I felt some connection to, but I could not put my finger on it. *Uncle Sid?*

"Good evening, sir. Welcome to The Black Wall Street Hotel," he said in a high voice, and with an inevitably warm glow. "You're overnighting, right?"

"I am," I confirmed.

"Wonderful." He clapped his hands in glee, showed me a large register and offered me a pen. It looked ancient. A relic. I also couldn't tell when last I had needed to sign my name at any

hotel. Real old-school. "We have you in the Tulsa Suite, sir."

I grinned. "*Suite?* All I wanted was a room and a bed. Wow! Listen, Mister ..." I waited for him to fill the gap. He did not. "I'm sure I haven't heard about this town before ..."

"Ah," the man smiled, "few have, but many are like you. Let me give you a quick history lesson." He paused, then explained: "November 1920, a town of five hundred residents. A thriving place of Black excellence, people doing well and just wanting to live their best lives. Unfortunately, that was not to be. Two brothers needed to defend themselves after being attacked by white men. Two of the white men died. In the ensuing carnage, the town was burned to the ground, and its nearly five hundred residents either killed or expelled. A massacre of the greatest proportions."

I listened. My chest hurt. "I never knew," I murmured. "I ... I'm sorry. So a new town was rebuilt?"

"It's okay, we overcame." The man smiled slyly and handed me a card key. That was as strange

as writing in a guestbook, the two incompatible. "What time would you like us to wake you, sir?"

"It's fine," I replied, making my way to the elevators, "the alarm clock in my head will get me up."

The man gestured and asserted: "It'll be our absolute pleasure."

"OK, if you insist," I called, not wishing to be ungrateful. "Seven AM." The doors slid open. I entered. "Good night. I did not catch your name …" He waved and smiled just as the doors glided shut.

My room, on the third floor four doors from the elevators, was definitely a suite. I wondered who was staying in the other rooms. African landscapes and floral and animal paintings adorned the walls, and the room was expansively furnished. More lavender. In the middle of the room stood a silver ice bucket on a glass-topped coffee table, a dark bottle propped up in its centre. For the second time that evening, my breath was taken away.

Unlacing my boots while seated on the bed, a ten-ton truck of tiredness crashed into me

and I collapsed, fully clothed. The soft mattress swallowed me whole, and burying me in its secure comfort. My sleep was the deepest and most peaceful I had ever had. There were no war nightmares.

Someone shook me, and slowly I opened my eyes and stared around. It took me a moment to comprehend where I was. I sat up suddenly, swinging my head to and fro. It could not be. I was looking at the barren landscape from my car. There were no buildings or smiling Black people, just a slow sun climbing into a blue sky, and dust devils dancing over the brown earth.

I closed and then reopened my eyes. Nothing had changed. I was not dreaming. I checked my watch: 7.01 AM. A whiff of something teased my nose, and I searched for the source. I knew the scent. It was right there on the passenger seat beside me, coming from a brown paper bag. There was a larger item, also wrapped in brown paper.

I opened the bag, and the smell of fried chicken blasted out. I retrieved the bag's contents one by one: a thick, white card cup that emitted a strong aroma of coffee, and a white cardboard box that

revealed the chicken and biscuits. I gasped and sat back, surveying the area again while switching on my GPS. As it booted up, I grabbed the larger wrapped object and tore at the paper. I glanced at my GPS; it showed nothing for miles. No blip. No solid dot. No town. No Ocoee. Holding my breath, I stripped each piece of brown paper away. A large wooden frame held a grainy photo. I recognised the wide street and buildings, and saw something I must have missed the night before. People stood in front of their stores just as when I drove past, looking in one direction, toward the camera, toward me. One stare, one united gaze. And just off centre, in front of Joe's Homestyle Eatery, was the big Black man. His eyes bore into mine. Smiling, he held up one hand as if waving.

I turned the frame and checked the back. It was plain except for a white label at bottom right. It read:

Ocoee, 1919. Joe McLeod, Mayor of Ocoee, stands in front of his newly opened store. The residents of Ocoee ...

The text went on to say that the McLeods were the most prominent family in the town. I started trembling. Now I understood the sense of familiarity. I had grown up with it. I experienced it at family reunions. I felt it in my elders, and in the way they hugged me. It was in the town's welcome. It was in my DNA, the unseen denominator that traversed time and space. They were me; *McLeod* was my last name.

I sat in my car, covered my face with my hands, and cried.

THE UNDERTAKER'S APPRENTICE

HANA GAMMON

I suppose that, when you dress up the dead and put them in the ground for a living, you must be prepared to answer a great many morbid questions, especially from children. Who chooses the clothes a corpse wears when it is buried? How are the mouth and eyes held shut? What is the point of embalming if the body is going to crumble into the earth after a few months, anyway?

These are the things that we children bombarded our little town's undertaker with whenever we chanced upon him in the street. Thinking back on it now, he was remarkably patient. We were an inquisitive lot, and he answered us calmly, without trying to wrap the

truth up to make it prettier, as we had come to expect from the other grown-ups in our lives. He explained to us at various street corners and crossroads, gesturing with his long, thin hands, how he stitched the lips of the dead and cleaned their flesh of its blood. He told us how he washed their faces and their hair, and how he folded their hands over their hearts before sending them down to be cradled by coffin wood in the dark, warm earth. He explained to us what he did and how he did it, and why, and we admired him greatly for his honesty. But the one question that we could never get him to answer was: *what's in the box*?

It was a large black box, rectangular and faintly polished. Some of us called it a "casket" rather than a box, which I suppose makes sense, but it was much plainer than a normal casket, with no hinges or handles as far as any of us could see. There did not seem to be any sort of seam between the two halves that would suggest where it might open; instead, it looked like one solid, sealed-up block of wood. It must have been hollow, though – and, many of us thought,

empty – because otherwise, I do not think that it could so easily have rested upon the shoulder of the young man who trailed about behind the undertaker wherever he went.

Just as we were fond of the undertaker, we children became rather fond of the young man, too. He didn't speak much, but when he did he was polite and clear in his words, and we could all see that he had great respect for the undertaker. We asked him once how exactly he had come to know the old man, and he had explained to us simply enough that he been taken in at a young age as an apprentice. Ever since, he had been drifting along in the man's shadow, watching and learning and carrying the big black box, which he explained the undertaker was too old to carry about by himself anymore. Having heard him explain the nature of his employment, we children had rather gleefully – and only once he was out of earshot – wondered aloud whether a person need only to look a certain way to become an undertaker in this town. The two men had the very same soft-stepping gait and the same pallid skin, the same thick dark hair –

although the undertaker's had turned more grey than black – and the same slate-brown eyes like rusty silver coins. They spoke in almost the same voice, and they smiled the same soft, serious smile; and when they rubbed their aching backs and shoulders, they did so with the same mannerisms, the same muted groans.

The undertaker's austere kindness and his patience in putting up with our morbid questions were not the only things that made him popular among us children. While all of us liked him, some of us – especially the little ones – had such a reverence that we began to see him as something far greater than just 'the old man who looks after people when they die'. I'm not entirely sure how it started, but there was a sort of trick, or rather a game, that the undertaker was willing to play with us. If one of us brought him something – anything, really – he would take it very gently into his long, sallow, wrinkled hands, and he would turn it about so that his skin seemed scarcely to touch the surface at all. Then, after these silent moments of consideration, he would hand it back and

tell you in a soft yet sure voice exactly what it was worth. He never spoke in terms of money. We were still too young then to have begun measuring worth in that way, anyhow. Rather, the undertaker had the uncanny gift of being able to equate the worth of things, sometimes abstract or even non-existent things, with each other. Sometimes, if we pestered him for long enough, he could even be convinced to trade.

One of us, a little girl, scratched an old, dry chicken bone out from her family's rubbish bin. She wandered the streets until she caught a glimpse of the undertaker, a tall dark shadow drifting between the buildings. I suppose, in her innocent childish ignorance, she thought the bone was a suitable gift for somebody in his profession. He took it from her, held it between his long, creased fingers, and – although he had been on his way from one side of the town to the other – he now stood very still for a long moment to examine the offering. Then he nodded and turned back the way he had come, vanishing with a billow of his black coat. He took the bone with him, along with his

apprentice, who walked on briskly and straight-backed under the weight of the long black box. The undertaker returned soon enough, and when he did, the chicken bone was gone. He carried between his fingers a broken eggshell. The little girl took it before she could say or ask him anything, and by the time she looked up again, he was gone. She kept the eggshell for a few months, hidden somewhere in her bedroom, until it became too brittle in the sun and the edges started to crumble.

On another occasion, while we were playing at the edge of the woods that skirted the town, one boy slipped while climbing an oak and snagged one of his cardigan buttons, ripping it off and tearing a huge gash in the cloth. We searched all through the long grass and the fallen leaves for the missing button, but it was lost. The little boy started to cry; his mother had spent months knitting him that cardigan. It was made of dark blue wool, soft and warm as the summer night sky, against which the golden buttons gleamed like stars. Now it was all beginning to unravel in wild, wiry strands around the jagged hole. I

remember feeling almost sick as I stood there watching the swiftness and ease with which all that work could be undone.

I think it had been my idea to go find the undertaker and see if he could help. The little boy, whose face was blotchy, red and tearstained, borrowed some other jumper from someone else and wiped his eyes on the oversized sleeves as we wandered through the streets. We checked every corner and alleyway for the sight of the two shadows.

Eventually we found him waiting at a crossroads, where we had chanced upon him many times before. We offered him the beautiful torn garment, which we had folded up as neatly as we could considering that it was crumbling into frayed threads. He would not even look at it, though, until it had been confirmed and reconfirmed that the boy himself had not been hurt. Then he took the ragged cardigan and unfolded it without ripping one more unravelling loop from another. He examined it, admiring the handiwork and the damage alike. He nodded and turned back the way he'd come.

And that was the last that any of us ever saw of that cardigan.

We found him in the same place a few days later, by which time most of us had already forgotten about the whole thing, at least until he beckoned to the little boy in the ill-fitting jumper to come forward. He put into the boy's outstretched hands a skein of midnight wool, the same in every way to that which had been torn to pieces in the woods, along with one golden button, glistening like a fallen star. Finally, he gave the boy a wide-eyed silver needle, fine but incredibly sharp. When he had gone, we speculated half-jokingly that it was the same sort of needle that he used for stitching the mouths of the dead.

The beautiful blue cardigan itself was nowhere to be seen. Perhaps it is still sitting, neatly folded and slowly disintegrating, in the corner of some hidden embalming room. How could the old man mend it now that he had given away his needle and thread? We all knew that we could not ask for it back. A week on, we were climbing trees just as carelessly as before, and after a month, most had forgotten that it had even happened.

The little boy kept wearing the borrowed jumper, which hung too loosely around his shoulders, at least for a few winters more until he outgrew it, and then he forgot about that as well.

I remember how a handful of us came up with a plan one spring while we were sitting around in the long grass with nothing to do. I cannot remember whose idea it was – I can scarcely recall who was there – but one way or another, we agreed that we should catch something, something living, and take it to the undertaker and find out what it was worth. I suppose we hoped to impress that old man whom we so much admired. Or perhaps we were trying to test the limits of what he was willing to take and to give. I remember that we argued for a long time over what our offering should be. Some of us wanted to dig under the dead leaves for worms, others to hook a fish from the creek and put it in his hands before it could stop gasping at the unwelcome air. One way or another, we ended up settling for a little brown sparrow that kept flitting in and out from the blossomed branches above our heads. It was small and delicate and its

song was simple but sweet – the perfect gift. The perfect offering.

We spent a long time devising a finicky trap of sticks and string. The hours flitted by, drawing us toward the dusk as we toiled. The sparrow kept dipping and chirping above our heads, unaware. At last the snare was set, carefully baited with a fat white grub we had pried from its bed between rotting folds of bark. We hid behind the bushes and we waited. We did not feel pity nor shame, much less guilt, at least not then as we sat quivering amid the dark leaves, watching our prey hop closer toward the snare.

Our plan worked. Can I say that it worked? I do not remember the sticks toppling, nor the beak snapping shut; and I do not remember a cry. But I remember the long silence afterward. I remember pushing my way into a crowded ring with the others, sensing their heartbeats and their breath, trying to see what they were seeing. I remember looking among the scattered sticks and seeing the dark, almost black blood spotting the grass. I remember shoving forward and fumbling amid the broken things, trying to

salvage what remained. The splinters of bone ground against each other under the skin, which I remember felt so soft and thin that my shaking fingers seemed to pose the danger of unwittingly pulling it apart.

I ran toward the town clutching the broken creature to my chest, with the others close behind. My shoes had been left back in the bushes – we had used the laces, I remember, for the snare – and my hair was tangled with sweat and leaves. My teeth were locked into a twisted grimace, features set. To anybody that saw me, I must have looked like some wild beast, but I did not care. All that mattered was that we find the undertaker. The sun had almost set by the time we caught sight of him. He was standing in the middle of the street, alone but for his young apprentice. Even if there had been people crowded on all sides, I still would have surged toward him. I thrust the mutilated thing into his hands and begged him to do what he could to forgive me, to forgive us all. He looked upon us with those soft, cold eyes as I spoke. While my wild breath escaped me and my words stuck

in my throat, he rested his firm, thin hand upon my shoulder. In a slow, soft voice that cut through the roar of the blood rushing in my head, he told me that it was not my fault, that it was nobody's fault, that it never was and never should be our weight to bear, nor our loss to mourn. It was only as he said this that I realised I had become hysterical with tears. My eyes had become puffy and creased into my face; my teeth were grinding into each other, and my cheeks were slick. My clothes smelled of earth. Mud and leaves clung to me. In hindsight, the bird could not have bled more than a thimbleful. But to a child, it seemed more than enough to stain both my hands up to the elbows. I must have looked like a walking nightmare. I suppose nothing much could unnerve the undertaker by that point. He simply nodded and cradled the shattered creature in one soft withered hand, and then handed me a handkerchief and told us to wait. He turned back into the street, clasping the bird to his chest, feeling its heart beating against his own, letting its blood invisibly speck his dark coat. His apprentice followed him, in

those days still nimble under the weight of the great black box.

It's hard to remember how long we waited. We waited and we watched, and the spring turned into summer. All of us grew a bit taller and some of us left the little town. Some returned only months or years later with new faces and new voices, and others simply never came back at all. Many of us forgot about the sorry incident with the bird. We had enough to worry about. Those of us who knew about the affair and could still remember could never think of a good enough reason to bring it up with anybody else who had been there. I believe we came very close to putting the whole incident behind us, until the undertaker reappeared toward the last days of that same summer. He stood silently at the edge of the woods behind the school with something in his hand. As we were walking out, tired and ready to go home after a long day, we saw the shape of the thing he held gleaming in the golden afternoon light, scattering sunbeams upon the yellowing leaves. When we came closer and stood there with him at the edge of the forest, we could

see that the thing he was carrying was, in fact, a birdcage. It was a beautifully crafted object, so arresting that we could all but stand there and look out from behind each other's shoulders, watching the light and the shadows rippling over the silver beams and the spaces between them. All that was missing was a door. The cage swung gently from his outstretched fingers, beautiful and bare and wide open without even a hinge to show where a door might once have been. With no way of refusing, we accepted the undertaker's exchange.

And we kept it. We could think of no reason why we should not keep it. Over that summer, over many more summers, the silver cage travelled from house to house. Sometimes it would find its way into a cupboard and stay there for months on end, or spend a season or two hiding in an attic or under the stairs. But it never properly disappeared. Each of us present that day had a turn eventually. The last time I saw it, the cage was sitting in the windowsill of the boy who had suggested we dig for worms beneath the leaves. For all I know, it is still there

today, gleaming in the morning sun and open to the world.

I remember seeing very little of the old undertaker after that. I used to wonder whether or not we had offended him in some way, and that, despite what he had told us that day, we would never really be forgiven and could never really clean what had happened from our clothes or fingernails. But I now see little reason for that to be true. Thinking back on it, I can see that his drifting away from us was really not so sudden a disappearance at all, just as we ourselves drifted further and further away from the centres of one another's lives. I do remember one day pedalling past a crossroads and becoming acutely aware that I had not seen his tall, grim shadow trailing through the streets for months, perhaps even years. His absence may have had nothing to do with what we did or could have done. He was a very busy man, after all, with more important things to worry about than answering silly questions about death and playing games with a group of children, especially ones who were not going

to be able to call themselves children for very much longer.

Who we started seeing more of, though, was the young man we had come to recognise as the undertaker's apprentice. Now that I think about it, it doesn't make much sense that we never saw the old man on his own, but that that boy seemed free to wander the streets alone almost at will, leaving his mentor to whatever grim, hidden chamber he dressed the town's dead in. Some of us scorned him for presumably abandoning his duties only to drift about like a lost ghost. As we grew older, some of us began to pity him. It was not because he looked lonely. These days, when we glimpsed him wandering the crossroads and street corners, there was often somebody following *him* for a change. I don't remember ever being there myself to see them pass. I suppose I always just missed them. Some of the others described the scene to me, though. I am told that he walked without a sound despite the weight on his back, bent over, hand outstretched, fingers curled softly around some old, gnarled hand. Always a new follower,

never the same one twice – at least, not initially. In order to be as good a guide as possible, he bowed his shoulders and cradled his great black box against his spine, under one arm. With the other hand he led whomever's turn it was to follow him. They crossed the road without stopping and without looking back, I am told, and then they simply vanished among the trees. One of us, a girl – the same girl, I think, who had, in her childish ignorance, gifted the undertaker a chicken bone all those years ago – once gathered three or four of us together behind the walls of our old school, amid the overgrown weeds and the smell of stale cigarette smoke. She told us with wide eyes that she had seen that boy's sallow hand fold around the coarse knuckles of her father as he was fixing a bicycle in the family's front garden. The older man had still been in his overalls, the sweat peaking his thin, soft hair into greyish spikes, when the undertaker's apprentice had led him away, bent-backed and with sure, silent steps. The girl had seen the two of them walking away and had hurtled toward them, shouting and shouting, until the echo of her

father's name rang through the streets. Neither had looked back. Both men had their eyes fixed somewhere beyond the shadows, hidden by the green-grey cloak of the trees snaking down toward the shallow valley. Her father had looked calm, she said, almost calmer than she had ever seen him before.

When she finished her story and could speak no longer, we all stood in silence, staring at her, waiting for somebody, anybody else, to speak.

I suppose the undertaker's apprentice must somehow have found his way back from that cloak of trees each time. If I can trust the others in what they say they saw, many of the times that he could be seen on the roads, he was with an old woman. Unlike the others, somehow, she kept following her guide back from amid the trees. It was as if he couldn't get rid of her even if he wanted to. Her back was bent almost into a hoop, they say, and she must once have been much taller than the small-boned shuffling shadow that she had become. Her skin had the same pale and almost sickly-sallow complexion as that of the young man and of his employer,

but if she had once shared their coarse, black hair, we couldn't tell, for time had bleached her curls as white and brittle as dry bone. Although she walked with slow and steady steps, she never fell behind her young guide, nor did she shuffle a hesitant half-step ahead of him. The two of them walked side by side, hand in hand, in the grey mornings and evenings when the sun seemed to be looking elsewhere. They whispered to each other in a language of soft-edged consonants that crashed gently over each other like fractured birdsong. Those that saw him swore that those were the only times they ever saw him without that great black box on his shoulders. Instead, he carried an umbrella in one hand – it always seemed either to be just about to rain or to have just finished raining when they walked together – which protected her clean, white curls from the dripping grey sky. And yet his shoulders still slumped, pressed down by the shape of the load even when only the empty space left by it remained. His spine curved deeper and deeper outward every time they caught a glimpse of him, year by year, until it looked as though he

would very soon become as closely bent toward the earth as she was.

I don't know. Like I said, I wasn't there to see any of it for myself. You could seek out one of the others who claimed to have seen them, only there aren't all that many of us left. But those of us who stayed behind saw less and less as the years went by of that old woman and that young man, and of course of the undertaker himself. Soon – and I'm sure I don't speak only for myself – it started to feel as though the old man were merely a half-forgotten dream or an imaginary playmate conjured up by us one summer at the edge of the forest when we were children.

I remember the last time I saw the undertaker. It is not all that long ago now. I came across him while I was walking alone early in the morning. The sunbeams were still cold and grey. I cannot remember where I was going or why, but I saw him there, crossing over from the city to the forest's edge. He was alone, and on his shoulders rested that great black box. He was bent like a wilted candle under the weight of it, his spine slumped, his head bowed, his black boots

shuffling silently through the rotting leaves. To see him like that stirred a pain through my bones the likes of which I can scarcely describe. Tears burned in my eyes, and I trampled toward him over the black earth, calling, trying to call – but I did not know what name to call, so instead I just wept. He glanced back at me, the lines of his face carved deep and twisted under the strain, but he did not stop. I kept calling. I kept pleading. I pleaded for him to put the box down, to leave it there at the border, or otherwise to give it back to his apprentice – who I knew suffered under the weight, but was at least younger and stronger. He did not listen. He stumbled onward, faltering but unstoppable, toward the trees.

Drunk with fear and a twisted and inexplicable anger, I rummaged back through my memories, trying to remember the first time I had met him, but I found nothing. He had always been there, and he had always known the worth and the weight of everything. And as I stood there with my face smeared with tears and my clothes stained by mud and grass, I cried through the grey stillness of the morning to the old man: "I

don't need to know what's in the box anymore! Please, just tell me what it's worth, and I'll give you anything in the world in exchange!"

He stopped then. I could hear the wood creaking against his shoulders as he turned to look at me. I do not know how his old bones could bear it.

"There is nothing you could give me that would cover its cost," he said in a soft voice that filled the forest's silence. "Even if there were, I would never let you have it. It is not a weight anyone so young should ever have to bear again."

And he turned again and shuffled away toward the shadows between the trees. They swallowed him up, leaving me alone at the edge of the forest before sunrise, before the birds began to sing.

OCEANS AWAY FROM MY HOMELAND

AGNES CHEW

1

My husband guides my finger over the curve of my breast. My heartbeat quickens. Then I feel what he's felt. Desire drains from my body. What was once familiar becomes foreign. I look down at my bare chest, unable to see the orb nestled in soft tissue that shifts beneath my fingertips.

2

In the days following the discovery of the orb, I cannot stop thinking of Marianne. She is a friend of a friend from back home, in Singapore. I don't know her well, but I know a story of hers.

A year ago, Marianne found a lump in her right breast. She ignored it for months in the hope that it would go away. It didn't. By the time she got it checked, it had grown to a degree that necessitated the removal of her entire breast. Marianne was only thirty-one when she was diagnosed with breast cancer.

I am about to turn thirty-two. Where I now live in Germany, the earliest available appointment to see a gynaecologist is three months later, in January. I fear it will be too late. I can't help thinking that if I were in Singapore, I would have been able to get an appointment within two weeks. I begin considering the pros and cons of flying home when my husband steps through the door to our apartment. I glance up from the wooden kitchen table at which I've been sitting all afternoon. As he shakes off his coat, he says he's called the gynaecology clinic and secured an appointment for me the following Monday at noon.

"They probably squeezed you in during their lunch break," he says.

"How did you do it?" I ask.

"I might have mentioned I'm a doctor, and that the lump needs closer examination." A sheepish grin spreads across his face. Despite the tautness in my chest, I find his smile is contagious.

3

A week passes. Seven nights of sleeplessness. Tonight is no different. In my left hand is my husband's. My husband, whose breathing deepens with each inhalation of air. Before my eyes I see the flickering of a thousand tiny lights, a thousand future possibilities. My mind drifts to Marianne.

What haunts me most about Marianne's story is the way her diagnosis hit 'pause' on the unrolling reel of her life. At that time, she had just quit her job at an investment bank, about to embark on a sabbatical to travel around the world. Her first stop was Beijing, from where she planned to take the Trans-Siberian Railway to Moscow. But on the day of her outbound flight from Singapore, she was rolled into an operating room. By the time she was supposed to have

landed in Beijing, she had lost a breast. Instead of the promised views of beauty and tranquillity framed by a train window, what awaited her was hormone treatment and chemotherapy. By the midpoint in her sabbatical, Marianne had lost the hair on her head, the bloom in her face and autonomy over her body and days.

But still she breathes. This is a fact we are meant to take comfort in.

Next to me, my husband lets out a snore. He lets go of my hand and turns to his side, away from me. I think about the novel I have spent the last four years writing, which will finally be released in eight months. I think about the changes Marianne has survived in eight months. I think about the bright lights that have been snuffed out, those that will be snuffed out.

I will not lie: it becomes increasingly difficult to breathe.

4

I have only been to the doctor once in the past three years I've been in Germany. My husband

frowns upon this. What he does not know is that it is also my only visit in the past decade. It had taken place during my first summer here, when I was still taking intermediate German classes, and my husband had accompanied me then to the clinic.

Much as I wish to erase the entire memory from my mind, there are certain details that remain with me from that day. The way the patients had spilled out from the single waiting room, down the cobwebbed steps, out the entrance of the faded, flesh-coloured building to form a human abscess of which I had become a part. That I had an appointment did not matter. There my husband and I stood, in the heat, for fifty-four minutes, staring at the cracks snaking across the length of the building, at the monstrous ants making their way across the tip of my dusty brown shoe.

The thudding of footsteps down the stairs announced the arrival of a nurse, who put an end to our wait. She frowned at her clipboard as she called out: *"Frau Yi … Yia … Ach, die Frau von Herrn Doktor Kupfer!"* Everyone turned to

stare at me. In her inability to pronounce my Chinese name, my identity had been reduced to the wife of my doctor husband. I wanted to tell my husband that even the flaxen-haired children before me had been called by their own names when their turns came, but I bit my tongue and followed them up the cobwebbed steps.

For the next two hours we spent in the clinic – which suffered from an acute case of poor ventilation – the people around me talked about me, over me, across me. Perhaps my appearance gave them the impression that I could not speak their language. They say the Germans are practical. And I, a mere subject.

5

Despite my deep aversion to visits to the doctor, I begin a countdown to my appointment with the gynaecologist. Five days. Four. Three. Two. One.

It is Sunday night, shortly before midnight. I lie in complete darkness, and my right hand slips under my cotton pyjama top. My fingers travel along the flat terrain of my stomach, then reach

the familiar rise of flesh. Like a pillow, the flesh yields under my finger pads. Before long, I feel that familiar pea-sized orb.

I ask my husband how I should describe the orb in German. I passed the advanced German proficiency test several months ago, but still I am unsure if it is enough to carry me through what is to come. I listen closely to the way the syllables leave his lips. Then I practise saying the words, as if reading from a script: I have a lump in my breast. *Ich habe einen Knoten in meiner Brust*.

I am repeating it a third time when my husband turns to me and takes my hands in his – his warm, mine cold. *"Alles wird gut,"* he says. *All will be well.* The same words with which I often reassure him.

"You don't know that," I say.

The night lamp comes on, bathing his thick brows and deep-set eyes in honeyed light. "Whatever happens, we'll go through it together." He squeezes my hands, and for a brief moment I feel a cool trickle of uncertainty seep out of me. Still, I know there are paths I must walk alone.

6

Monday morning. I am about to leave the apartment to catch the bus when a message from my mother pops up on my phone. It's the same question she's been asking all week. *Is my husband accompanying me to the gynaecologist today?* Again I reply in the negative. I'd told her yesterday that most of the doctors in his department are down with illness or away on holiday, that he won't be able to get away from work. I pull back my shoulders as I open the door. But it is too late; my confidence wavers.

Forty minutes later, I step off the bus. With an hour to spare, I head toward the nearest bookshop. It is strange to consider that I used to always be late in Singapore – a habit I've gradually come to shrug off the longer I live in this land of punctuality. As I make my way to the ENGLISH FICTION section, my phone lights up with a message from my husband, asking how I am feeling.

Ich habe Angst, I type back. In German, the word *angst* refers not to the vague anxiety one

feels about the state of the world but rather fear. A literal translation: *I have fear.* I weigh the words against the English equivalent of *I am scared*, and an undercurrent of comfort washes over me. Perhaps it is the subconscious knowledge that this fear onto which I am holding in this present moment could leave me in the next, would eventually pass me by. That it does not define me. That I am more than my fears, more than a pea-sized orb nestled in the left of my chest.

Ich schaffe das, I tell myself. *I can do it.*

There is no reply from my husband. He must be busy with his patients. I slip my phone into my bag and head towards the shelves of books. For the next thirty minutes, I flit in and out of luminous, imaginary worlds, and it almost distracts me from my impending ordeal.

7

At the entrance to the gynaecology clinic, I ring the bell. Once, twice, multiple times. But each time I try to push the door open, it does not yield. Only after eight minutes, when someone

leaves the clinic, am I able to enter. I notice the air-conditioning unit as I step inside, which briefly reminds me of its ubiquity in Singapore, though this one lies quiet now that summer is over. As I walk toward the reception desk, the door behind me clicks open. I glance back. A red-faced woman whose stomach is swollen with life comes in. She is panting from the exertion of climbing one flight of stairs. I am likewise breathless, though for other reasons.

I practise enunciating the last name of the gynaecologist under my breath until it is my turn to speak to the bespectacled receptionist. She does not return my smile, but I tell myself not to take offence. I hand her my health insurance card, fill in a form, evade the question of when I had last been to a gynaecologist. She then directs me to the third waiting room at the end of the corridor.

I take a seat. Here, I am alone.

Inhale, exhale. I focus on the way my lungs inflate and deflate.

Last night I dreamed of my grandmother, whom I haven't seen in five years. It is only

later, when the gynaecologist asks if there is a history of cancer in my family, that I recall my grandmother died from cancer, that I had not been around to hold her hands when she took her last breath. But for now this fact eludes me, and the details of my dream become hazier the more I try to recollect them. All I remember is the look of pure joy on my grandmother's face. The way the laugh lines that fanned out from her eyes nearly touched when she smiled. The way her affection flowed from her etched palms into the crevices between my fingers, my bones.

I wonder if this is a sign – a good sign.

Without realising it, I have folded my hands together in prayer the same way my grandmother had taught me to when I was a child, as I stood before the altar in her two-bedroom flat, barely tall enough to see the glowing tips of the joss sticks she had planted in the incense pot. I no longer remember the words of the sutra, but I remember how comforting it felt to be in her presence. By instinct, I bow my head and close my eyes.

Here I am, sitting in an empty waiting room oceans away from my homeland, from the safety of my girlhood. But perhaps I am, after all, not alone.

8

"Frau Vee?"

Wee, I correct under my breath. Unlike most of the women here, I did not take my husband's surname after marriage.

I stand and walk toward the voice. It feels like a test, and I will myself not to trip. *One step at a time,* I tell myself.

The gynaecologist is dressed entirely in white. She introduces herself, but I daren't meet her gaze. I am told to close the door behind me, so I do. Then the questions begin. I want to express my preference to hold our conversation in English; it is at the tip of my tongue, but instead I swallow it.

And so we continue in German – my third language, one which I have only begun to acquire

in adulthood. Everything feels one level removed; one language further, less real. Perhaps that is why, when encouraged by the gynaecologist, I agree to do a routine Pap smear on the spot, in addition to the ultrasound that will follow. I do not believe myself, do not recognise myself. I answer her questions, follow her instructions. I remove my underwear, spread my legs on a tilted chair. Then I peel off my top, my bra, lie down with my arms over my head.

It is only when the coldness of the ultrasound gel stings my skin that I realise this is it: the purpose of my visit. I clasp my fingers together. If I shut my eyes tightly enough – could I pretend I didn't exist? But my eyes are wide open, staring at the screen. Dark, unknown waters emerge as the wand glides over my left breast. The images, swirled with white, appear murky, obscure. Then the wand stops. And I spot it at once: a black blob amid the foamy waves. The orb. My breath catches in my throat. The gynaecologist in white says nothing.

I wait, and the wand moves on.

9

I step out of the clinic into dappled light. A gust of wind rushes past, stripping a nearly bare tree branch of its yellowing leaves. Above me echo the yelps of migratory geese. I take a gulp of autumnal air, filling my lungs with the scent of decay. I reach for my phone and skim through the messages from my husband and my mother.

For now, no one else is privy to what the gynaecologist has said to me earlier in the consultation room. For now, no one else knows that there is not just one orb in my breast, but several of them. Bubbles of darkness lurking in the chalky waters of my breast tissue. The one that precipitated this visit to the clinic is the largest of them, measuring a centimetre and a half wide.

Soon my husband calls and I tell him the news. Then I send my mother a long message, telling her the same. When I read her reply, I begin to cry. It does not matter that I am a grown Asian woman, walking down a European street with tears streaming down my cheeks. I read my

mother's message again, and again. She wishes she could have been here with me. I think back to eleven years ago, when she had to undergo surgery to remove a fibroid in her uterus. The same uterus in which she had carried me for the first nine months of my existence. Where had I been then? In London, on a student exchange programme. What had I wished for then? That the fibroid didn't exist, that I wouldn't have to return home prematurely.

The tears do not stop. It hurts to breathe.

10

I close the door to the bathroom. As I peel off my clothes, my fingers brush over gummy traces of ultrasound gel near the pit of my arm. In the mirror, I catch a grimace on my face.

You should be thankful, I urge myself. Thankful that the bubbles of darkness lurking within my chest have not been classified by the gynaecologist as sinister. Thankful that I now have another six months to live before the next check-up. Thankful for the steadfastness of my

husband, my mother, my grandmother, in spite of my shortcomings.

But there is something I have not told them.

Within my womb lies another orb the size of a blueberry, whose life is at my mercy.

LECH, PRINCE
AND THE NICE THINGS

RUE BALDRY

"You know who you look like?" he asks. I run my trowel through the muck in my bucket. Needs a touch more water. "Prince. That's who. He's the spit of him, right?"

A couple of brickies and a sparky hum noncommittally.

I look nothing like Prince. I'm a short Black man, that's all.

There's a weighted pause until someone says, "Yeah, that's right, Boss."

"That's what I'm gonna call you then," the boss tells me. He calls the lumpy Welsh brickie "Tom Jones" too, though he won't attract many Delilahs.

Nobody's surprised when, instead of answering, I splash in enough water to sort my muck out; they expect plasterers to be taciturn. I've been told by more people than I can be bothered to remember that they couldn't stick the monotony of my job. Its meditation suits me, though. And I'm bloody good.

They've been renovating this basement for three months. Down here it's a building site of pokey rooms off a big cellar space with stone stairs down the middle. The house is Victorian or Georgian, something like that. Not that you'd know from the shiny, modern entrance hall I glimpsed when the boss opened the front door for me this morning.

He said, "I'm Trevor, but you can call me 'Boss'." Apparently that's not a racist thing, because all his builders do it. I'd wondered, because he'd already told me, "I didn't realise you'd be ... like, on the phone you didn't sound –" but thought better of finishing.

Unsurprisingly, I'm the only Black guy on the team.

Until lunch, I face the wall, sweeping my arm from side to side, smooth and soft, letting my mind peel off to tangents. With plastering, you never really work with anyone else. They do their own stuff in their own groups. Closest anyone gets is the chippy fitting skirting boards. On this job, that's a middle-aged Polish guy.

"Don't mind him. No English," says Boss. "I call him 'Lech'." He pronounces it like the start of *lechery*, though I'm sure it should be a hard K.

Lech puts a length of new skirting up to my wall and gets sandpaper out of his pocket, but knows better than to start using it near wet muck. He backs out. I skim.

Boss is still talking. "Like that Lech Walesa. You'd be too young to know about him."

I have read about the Gdańsk Shipyards, actually.

Most of the men go out to McDonald's for lunch, but I've brought a packup. In the back-yard Portaloo, I soap up to my elbows, then *squirt-squirt-squirt* the little tap. Coming back indoors, I spot a pair of grubby jeans heading

up the steep back stairs, which must have been built for servants. There's no dustsheet on that staircase, marking it out of bounds.

I edge forward, see that it is Lech ascending them. There's nobody else about, so I stick my boots behind the door, silently follow him. It's easy to creep soundlessly on this thick, red carpet. I can't hear Lech. I think I'm following a trace of his body odour, but it might be my own. I keep my elbows tucked away from the pale cream walls and glossy black banister.

Off the first landing is a glass-panelled door. I cover my hand with clean sweatshirt cuff pulled out from under my overalls, to twist the shining doorknob. The wood swishes open with minimal resistance into a dark corridor smelling of rose and lemon – or, rather, the scents they sell under those names.

Soft light and a heavy splashing sound cascade from an open door. Approaching it reveals a brass shower rail, then a heavy, matching lever and showerhead behind an etched glass door; there's a claw-footed bath perched on a tray of unnaturally symmetrical stones in the middle of

the room. Lastly, there's Lech's grimy back view, the source of the prolific pissing noise.

I stand still and, as far as I can tell, silently, but when Lech has finished with the loo and turns, dick still in hand, he does not look the least surprised to see me. He walks to a satin swag of curtain patterned in shades of turquoise that perfectly match the striped wallpaper and wipes his penis on it, giving me only the faintest smile.

I nod solemnly in return, stepping to one side so he can pass me while tucking himself away. I follow him down the back stairs. There's still plenty of time left to eat my sandwiches.

That night, Lisa wants to go to a bar, but neither of us have been paid yet; so instead we sit on my bed, eating pasta out of the saucepan and watching *Pottery Throwdown* until I distract her by stroking her thighs. She smells of Surf fabric softener and the Colonel's secret recipe.

In the morning there isn't enough time for both of us to shower, and no room to get in together, so I let her be the one to wash and I carry her scent in to work on me.

* * *

"Who does he look like, eh? Prince, isn't it? The singer from the Eighties?"

I am flicking subtle window trowel scrapes round the tiny high windows while Boss gives a basement tour to a white bloke in a suit.

"Glad to see you're plastering at last." The voice is younger than I expected, and not so posh.

"Prince, say hello to Gordon Politan-Ellis. That's his wall you're slopping muck all over."

I don't slop.

I turn to greet Mr Politan-Ellis, because I want a look at him. Tall, tanned, maybe mid-thirties. His temples look like they ought to be distinguished grey, but he's not there yet. His suit is as weighty and well-cut as you'd expect, with a glint at his cuffs, shined shoes, a thick watch and a spiced, clean fragrance I have to hold myself back from deeply inhaling.

I nod at him.

"We need to finish as quickly as possible," he says.

I stick my window trowel in the bucket, fold my mortar stand and move to the main room. The window work isn't as finished as it could be, but there's no point providing perfection for someone who won't appreciate it.

Lech is working in here. We don't look at each other until lunchtime, when we wait for the rest to go, slip off our boots and go back to the bathroom. While he's pissing, I lift the brass cap off the shower drain, peel plaster from my arms and drop it down. I turn the heavy lever of the shower. There's a pause, then warm water pelts down from the oversized head.

I check Lech's reaction; there isn't one.

Leaving my overalls, socks and sweatshirt on the marble tiles, I step onto the shower tray in my underpants. The hard stream works clean rivulets over my skin. Diluted plaster spouts from my fingers. The permanent ache across my shoulders submits.

Through steam, I see Lech's arm at the shower door, offering me a block of something amber. It is the size of a half brick, with a stalk of rosemary and dark speckles embedded through. It might

be an ornament or paperweight, except that when I take it, it's slippery. Lech has gone before I can thank him. I sniff. Definitely soap.

I rub it over my arms. Its edges are still sharp. I foam it between my palms, use that to lather my neck, chest, legs. I clean the muck off the lever. Finally, I shove the bar into my underwear, rub it front then back, then ease my waistband to rinse. There's a soft *clunk* when I stop the water.

I look for a towel. Should have thought of that earlier. None on the heated rail or the brass hooks. They must have packed them away when they moved out for the duration of the building work. No bathmat either, so I'll have to be careful.

I shake as best I can, place the soap on my pile of clothes for now, gingerly tiptoe to the landing. The wet fabric of my pants clings awkwardly and water drips down my leg hair.

I head toward a chandelier, but before I reach it there's a door. It's not locked.

Folded on the bare mattress of an ornate double bed is a set of bed linen: thick, crisp, ivory-white, smooth. I press my damp palms onto the top sheet. A movement from behind

startles me, but of course it's just Lech. He is holding the fluffiest, whitest towel I've ever seen.

While I'm drying myself with it, he runs his dick over the edge of the stack of bedding.

I blot my underpants one last time, hold up the towel. He tucks himself away as I follow him along a wide landing overlooking the entrance hall, then into a much larger bedroom. He passes its four-poster, eyeing the lace drapes through a doorless arch to a narrow room with a good view of the landscaped back garden. Its deep greens catch me for a second. A wave of goose pimples brings me back to the dressing room.

One long wall is entirely mirrors. Opposite them sit a pale wood dressing table topped with three adjustable mirrors, a tallboy in slightly darker wood with a shaving mirror on it and a freestanding, full-length mirror with an ornately carved frame.

Lech slides back one of the wall mirrors to reveal shelves heaped with thick fabrics in esoteric tones. I fold my towel into a geometric bundle identical to the other bath towels.

Lech lifts the top half dozen of the stack and I manoeuvre in the damp interloper.

He returns to the lace bed curtains, reaching into his fly as I leave to get dressed.

There's no time to eat my sandwiches before the builders and sparkies get back, so I spend the afternoon hungry, with moist underwear. Every time I move my arm, though, I'm breathing in rosemary and vanilla.

From the top deck of the bus on the way home, eating my lunchtime butties and reading *Hegemony or Survival*, I spot Lech clumping across the side road by William Hill with his tool bag across his back. Despite straining round, I can't see where he is headed.

I exchange texts with Lisa. She is going to babysit for her sister tonight.

Soon as I'm in my bedsit, I undress and chuck my clammy boxer briefs into the laundry bag. I should have showered naked. I can't see Lech being bothered; he has kept his knob in his hand for most of the past two lunchtimes. I drape my overalls across the one radiator, crotch central, hoping their blobs of plaster won't scrape its

chipping paint and that they'll be fully dry by morning.

My duvet cover feels scratchy and thin when I sit naked on the bed. Its print has faded. I hadn't noticed before.

My forearms, feet and calves still smell great. Not my armpits. I should have looked for deodorant in that dressing room. I bet Gordon's got nice stuff. Cologne, too, like I smelled on him. I bend down, getting my nose as close as possible to my groin's raw, puckered, impression of underwear. Pretty fragrant.

To keep the smell from drifting off, as much as for the warmth, I snuggle under the duvet.

I text Lisa, ask if we can video call. She says she's too busy with the kids. I tell her I'm naked. She replies, *In that case definitely not!*

● ● ●

Next day, I look through the tallboy. In the top drawer are jewellers' boxes, silk pocket squares, tweezers, toenail clippers and – what I was hoping for – tiny glass fragrance bottles.

I sniff each one. Woody, leathery, citric ...
I can't find the spicy one he was wearing
yesterday morning, but there's a bergamot and
cardamom, which I like even better. I dab it
along my clavicle and unbutton my overalls to
anoint my belly button.

Lech leaves the cocktail dresses he's been
marking to go through the jewellery boxes,
replacing each one exactly when he's done with
it. Cufflinks, tie pins, watches in silver, gold,
platinum and leather, all their faces studded
with precious stones. He wraps a metallic link
strap round his dick.

I stick one of the slick, pastel hankies down
the front of my open overalls to rub it about a
bit. Lech watches me, nodding approval, smiling
slightly. I fold it, pick off a hair, replace it.

There are just three pairs of socks in the next
drawer. Cashmere. Imagine the socks he *did* take
with him. I unroll the racing-green pair, turn one
inside out and shove it into my arse crack. Lech
jerks his bare bum across the carpet like a dog
with worms, his angular image multiplied in all
the mirrors.

We close the drawers, adjust our dress to disguise ourselves as respectable, respectful workmen, head down the stairs. I'm halfway through my ham and cheese bap when the crew get back.

That evening, when I see Lech through the bus window, I hop off to spy on him from the bus stop. He goes in the door beside the Londis. It has a dozen, unnamed doorbells. I get on the next bus.

Lisa doesn't mention the cologne, which heats up while I'm making love to her.

* * *

Next morning, there's a red car parked down the side of the house. It's one of those that's the size of a minibus, but there's only actually room for four passengers. It's so tall I have trouble looking in to work out what the sound system is.

"Get away from my car!" The supercilious blonde might be in her thirties, but it's hard to tell through the layers of gloss on her face and

the tight tone of her body. Her hair is as brittle as her spiked heels.

I escape down the narrow passage she's left us to reach the back door.

"Oh no, you don't!" She clips every consonant. "I'll call the police."

I'm in plaster-specked overalls. There's building work in the cellar. I don't need to explain, don't even know who she is.

Tom Jones and Vin Diesel, having a smoke against the Portaloo, are chuckling their heads off. I can't look at them.

Boss speeds past us. "I'm ever so sorry. Estelle. Mrs Politan-Ellis. Nothing to worry about. He's with us. I know what it looks like."

Lech stands unsmiling, just inside the back door, arms folded. I can't meet his eyes. Boss is asking Estelle Politan-Ellis whether or not I'm the spit of Prince.

For most of the morning I shut myself inside the smallest cellar annex. I soothe myself by sweeping creamy muck over then back, left then right, over then back. At some point I hear wheels move off above my head.

I'm startled when Lech opens the door. God knows where my mind had taken itself. My upper arm aches.

He tugs my elbow. I lay down trowel and hawk, go with him. There are still a couple of men around. They smirk at me. Lech gets hold of my hand at the bottom of the stairs, keeps it until we get into the dressing room. I'd rather have a bath.

He opens a dressing-table drawer to show me a tangle of necklaces, makeup, hairpins, rattling acrylic nails and gruesome objects which could be dead spiders or false eyelashes. It's the messiest thing I've seen in the whole house, nothing like Gordon's neat handkerchief collection. Lech selects a lipstick, rotates its base. Most of a newish burgundy-brown stick rises. He grins at me. I'm not ready to smile yet.

Inevitably, he pulls out his limp, pale cock to run the lipstick round and round its head. My mouth does twitch upwards then.

He offers me a coral pink one, which would look great on Lisa, but could only ever make Estelle look even older. I shove it down my pants.

Lech pats both sticks back into shape before returning them and taking out a couple of liquid eyeliners. He paints eyes onto his shaft. I paint under my balls. Once we've played with concealer, blusher brushes and a powder puff between my buttocks, I'm grinning, too.

I'd still like that bath. I take a towel and a bodywash, leaving Lech to put things back to rights. Well, back to the untidy state we found them in.

* * *

Lisa doesn't stay over that night, has to get back because it's her dad's birthday the next day. I've never met her family. I wonder whether that's because she hasn't told them I'm Black. I've been with her for eight months. I don't know how to ask her.

I drag prongs across walls all the next morning, while my mind circles. There's only two people living here (I may not chat, but I do eavesdrop), so I can't see why they need all these rooms.

What can be on the top floor? Why do they want this cellar habitable, too?

I'm done with scarifying just before lunch. I've eaten my sandwiches before the rest of the team leave.

I go up beyond the first floor. Lech watches me through its glass-paned door. The prongs of the scarifier in my front pocket poke me. I don't know why I've brought it.

There's no door separating the attic floor from the servants' stairs. Turning the last corner, I get hit by the glitz of sunlight through veluxes, which is bouncing between mirrors and chromed gym equipment. I can't imagine anyone working out in this glare. Maybe that's what the cellar's being converted for. Would be easier to buy blinds.

Their free weights don't pose me any challenge. Last thing I need in the middle of a working day is more arm exercise, anyway. Running the scarifier lightly over the tread of the running machine, I can't see how to connect them, so I sit my bare arse on the exercise bike, but only to keep up tradition. There must be thousands of

pounds' worth of stuff here, but most of it isn't very interesting.

The rowing machine could be promising. I gather my train of overall to shuffle to it. My socked feet fit nicely into the footholds, as do my naked bum cheeks on the sun-warmed seat; I pull back the handles. There's a swishing noise of real water.

When Lech arrives, I'm pissing into the hole on the side of the tank attached to the machine.

Lisa texts that she wants to stay over tonight. I don't reply.

I spend the afternoon scarifying ceilings. My neck and shoulders are killing me by the time I leave. I'd love to soak them in a big bath with pointless spherical pebbles under it, but have to make do with my black-spotted, cramped shower.

Two wet strides land me on my bed. I read the same Brian Pearce paragraph three times before it makes sense, put the book down and channel-hop for a while, then finally answer Lisa's text by suggesting that I stay at hers for a change. She doesn't reply.

* * *

Next day, because it's Friday, lunch is early and short, so we can down tools at two-thirty. Boss herds us out and makes a great show of locking up. I rinse my arms at the standpipe, make him wait by the back gate with his clutch of keys until all the plaster is off. I don't flick my wet arms at him.

Lisa texts when I'm on the bus. The first few words include *sorry*. I don't read the rest of it. If Lisa saw a Black man looking at her car, what would her assumptions be? Lisa hasn't got a pot to piss in, never mind a flash car, but none of her family have met me. Eight months.

I grin to myself, imagining taking a dump in that claw-footed bath on the pebbles. I think through all the potential consequences of actually doing it. Still tempted.

I didn't know I was going to, but I get off at the stop opposite the Londis. I cross the diesel-gusting road, go inside. The washing powder smell switches my brain back on as the door's bell chimes. A woman watches from behind the counter.

I stride down the middle aisle to stand purposefully in front of their toiletry shelves. I bet Gordon and Estelle never shop at Londis. I bet there's not a thing in here they'd ever deign to own. I try to smell a bar of soap through its wrapper. I don't know why I'm here. If Lech walked in I probably wouldn't even speak to him, don't know if I'm here because I'm hoping he will be.

My phone chimes an alert into the overlit air. I daren't check whether or not the shop assistant is watching me. I don't want cheap soap. This isn't a museum; if I don't buy anything it'll look like I'm shoplifting. Toothpaste. I don't need it yet, but it's not like it goes off. I get a bag of Brazil nuts off the reduced section on the way past.

The shopkeeper tells me to have a good evening when she gives me the receipt.

Lisa has texted again. Three more times, actually. Her pay just came through, so she wants to take me to Xiangqi, a new Chinese on her side of town. She suggests we meet at her place.

The bus comes. There's another text alert as I'm sitting down. Her address. I reply *ok 7.30.*

After a long but soapless shower, I can't face using any of my four-for-three body sprays. I do wear my newest shirt and cleanest jeans. My overalls form a meniscus on the laundry bag. I always go to the laundrette on a Sunday.

The house at the address Lisa gave me has rusted-metal heaps on its eczemic front lawn. I double-check the text. No bell, so I rap on the bubbled-paint door.

Her neat clothes and hair contrast against grubby wallpaper and stairs with filled plastic carrier bags on every step. We grin at each other. She gives me a soft kiss on the cheek, steps out of the house.

"That him, is it?"

Lisa's face sours. She shrugs at me and walks back in.

He sits in a beige armchair with uneven patches of grey, wearing a vest and tracksuit bottoms, nursing an overflowing ashtray. Beside him is an identical empty chair with an identical ashtray. The TV plays a muted horserace.

"We meet at last!" he says, extending a bluish arm. His face is split with a warm smile.

"This's my dad," Lisa mumbles.

While I'm shaking his tacky hand, he says, "Pleased to meet you."

I believe he is.

"And you," I reply, meaning it.

"Finally," he adds, looking sideways at Lisa. "Anyone'd think she was ashamed of us." He shifts his weight forward, pressing a hand onto the rubbed-flat arm of the chair, begins rising.

"We better get going," Lisa says.

Her highly polished court shoes look superimposed on the cellophane-and-hair-streaked vinyl flooring.

"See you later," I tell her old man.

Walking down the road, I hold her pristine fingers. Her neck is pink in patches. She is avoiding my eyes.

"He seems nice," I say.

She shrugs. "Can we go to yours after?"

"Of course."

The food is sweet and greasy, but I've had worse. Lisa's lipstick wipes onto the wineglass with her first sip. Lisa deserves quality. I'd like to steal her one of Estelle's. Wonder if she'd even

notice. Then I remember where some of those lipsticks have been, and put them out of my mind.

● ● ●

We make tipsy love in my bedsit, with soy-sauce kisses. The scratch of bobbled sheet wakes me in the early hours. Thoughts stop me from getting back to sleep.

When Lisa wakes, she has a shower. I'm aware she's having to stand between the cracked tiles of my scratched-up bathroom. I wish we could share a deep, enamelled tub. I'm not bothered about the pebbles, and it could sit against the wall. We'd relax in there all morning, topping up the hot water.

I check emails on my phone. One asks me to quote for re-plastering the whole downstairs of one of those villas that got flooded. That's got to be a few weeks' work. They want it sized up in the next few days, which would mean taking time off from the Politan-Ellis job, so I don't reply.

I haven't even seen most of their rooms yet. I want to touch everything they own. I look from my damp-stained ceiling to the foxed library books piled between discoloured patches on the windowsill, to the swollen chipboard edge of the headboard. I close my eyes.

My phone rings. The bloke calling sounds flustered. He got my number off a friend of Lisa's sister. His plasterer's broke his wrist, and took four days to let them know. I ask how much he was charging.

When he's told me, he adds, "But we'll pay more if you can start soon. We can't use the bath or shower 'til it's done. It's been weeks and we've got kids. Got to get the plaster on so we can seal –"

I say, "I'm on this other job."

"Please, mate. You'd be a life saver. I'm a nurse. I've been trying to dry me uniform in the kitchen, but that's full of all the bathroom stuff and –"

I suppose I could rush through the Politan-Ellis job. Gordon doesn't care about craftsmanship, after all.

"I'll have a look this afternoon."

"Thank you so much."

It doesn't really matter, but I ask anyway: "Would anyone else be in the house while I was working?"

I don't know whether I'm disappointed or relieved that they would.

I may not be a Politan-Ellis, but I can afford new bedding. I search on my phone. There's a lot of choice. Silk sounds luxurious, but it might be slippy. But then, that might be nice. There must be a reason why that's not what the Politan-Ellises have. I'll check the labels on their bedsheet stack on Monday.

"Who was on the phone?"

Lisa curls into me, smelling of synthetic grapefruit, warm, damp, and naked. Clean.

"A job. Work's getting regular. And they're giving you more shifts, too, right?"

"Mmhm."

No reason not to say it, so I do. "Maybe nearly at the point where we could look for a place together? What d'you think?"

"You want us to live together?"

It's been eight months. "Sure."

"Couldn't I just move in here?"

"Here? But it's a shithole."

She sits up, laughing. "I love this place. You've seen where I'm living. You keep things so nice here."

"Be nicer with you living in it."

● ● ●

I reply to the email about the villa, offer to look at it before work on Monday. I write their quote on the bus, get that sent off and reply to an email from the nurse asking for my bank details before I've even walked past the Portaloo on the Politan-Ellis patio.

At lunchtime, I check the bed linen labels in the spare bedroom. Egyptian brushed organic cotton. It has a nap like suede. Lech walks in on me, comes close. I lean away because I'm expecting him to wipe his pecker on the pillowcases again.

"She's coming up here now," he says. Perfect English. A bit of an accent, but it isn't from anywhere further east than South Shields.

We scuttle down the back stairs. I'm tying my bootlaces when a light comes on behind the

glass-panelled door above me. My stomach's too clenched for my sandwiches. I can't think through what evidence we've left up there. Hands shaking, I mix new muck.

In a darkened alcove, alone with the sped-up slap-and-slide of fresh plaster over scraped wall, my pulse slows, temperature drops, heart returns to normal. I stay as late as I can.

I see Lech crossing the road when I'm on my way home. I stay on the bus.

Lisa is lighting scented candles in our bedsit. I'm glad I never found any of the Politan-Ellises' candles. No doubt their expensive fragrances would have spoiled me for enjoying these. She has arranged our mugs by colour on the shelf over the kettle, mine mingling in the same stacks as hers. Her oversized hardback on ceramics photography leans against my library books. We order a set of brushed-cotton bedding from John Lewis in cool grey.

● ● ●

I finish the second coat of plaster the next

morning. It's thin and sloppy, but I gather my tools together anyway. Diesel asks me if I'm off already. I don't reply. I tell Boss I'm done when the rest have left for their lunch. It's only the second time I've spoken to him, so I've never had to call him anything to his face, which pleases me. He wants to write me a cheque, but I don't trust his accounting, so I wait on the dustsheet protecting the back hall while he goes round the corner to a cashpoint.

Lech watches me through the glass panels of the door off the first flight of back stairs. I'm not tempted to follow him. I'm busy thinking up nice things I'll be able to buy for Lisa. I wave to him; he nods in return.

When I pocket Boss's banknotes, he doesn't thank me for my work, so I don't thank him for the pay.

I go to the nurse's house to get started on plastering his bathroom, so he'll be able to wash his kids.

KILINOCHCHI

HIMALI MCINNES

When Nisha performs the burial ceremony for AJ, her twenty-six-year-old son, she has to imagine his body lowering into the earth. Without a body, cremation is impossible. This ceremony, instead, is a commingling of the Christian traditions practiced by Nisha's husband Sam and the ancient Hindu rites of her own ancestors. A pot of ghee, a spoonful of raw honey, sandalwood oil. A garland of marigolds sewn together, the flowers bought earlier from the Cornwall Park Superette on Great South Road. Psalm 23, written out by Nisha on a sheet of paper pressed with petals. *Even though I walk through the valley of the shadow of death, I will fear no evil, for you are with me.* A rendition of "Amazing Grace", one of Nisha's favourite hymns, plays on her iPod. AJ wasn't religious,

but since he left three years ago to fight his war of liberation, Nisha finds herself turning toward holy things for comfort. And now her son is dead, his mother's prayers spent. She refuses to think that AJ's body might be in hundreds of pieces somewhere in the northeast of a tiny island in the Indian Ocean. Instead, she imagines him whole, perfect, hands clasped as if in prayer. She does not cry, yet her skin prickles with the sense that someone is watching her, keeping time with her; but when she turns around, she sees no one.

She comes from a line of fire, this much she knows. Nisha is Tamil, yet *Tamil* or *Sinhala* are just superficial distinctions to her. Dig deeper for descriptions more resonant with meaning: *merchant, poet, warrior, peasant*. Thousands of couplings, some volitional, some forced, across the still heat of centuries. She comes from a line of people who embrace uncertainty, the spirit world, the existence of knowledge beyond touch, taste, sight or sound. Nisha's great grandmother and great-great-grandmother, her shimmering ghostly companions since childhood, are as real to her as the living. Death has had no

impediment on their constant catty comments: *You are looking too fat, Nisha, time to cut down ... We know a nice Tamil boy from the up-country station, ask your Appa to make a proposal before you become an old crone ... Ferment the ground rice batter for three days, get the hopper pan sizzling, serve with hot hot sambol; no man will be able to resist your palappum.* They follow her to New Zealand. Of course they do; they wouldn't allow her and AJ to leave without them.

Sam doesn't believe in what he calls "batshit nonsense". He's an engineer who dwells inside the solidity of tar-seal, the gravity of mortar, the fissile tension and compression across a bridge's span. *You don't know what you don't know,* Nisha wants to say to him. When she tells him she is going to have a burial ceremony without confirmed news of AJ's death, Sam shouts at her:

"You can't possibly know that that idiot is dead, Nisha! Until we have proof, I'm not wasting my energy."

Nisha cups soil to her lips, whispers words of blessing in Tamil, throws dirt over AJ's invisible body. *I forgive you.* She folds the marigold wreath

inside, carefully covering the hole with more soil. There are no other mourners on this windy day in her Auckland garden. Only wax-eyes chittering and commenting – her favourite bird, olive-green feathers and bright eyes stencilled with silver, so small an entire family can fit inside her cupped hands; their te reo Māori name, *tauhou* ("new arrival"), Nisha's constant story despite fifteen years in her adopted land. Rain settles like tiny diamonds on her hair. The prickly presence stands so close she can feel it breathing.

"How do you know AJ is dead, Nish?" Annie asks. Annie lives next door. "I mean, how do you know the silly bugger hasn't finally come to his senses and decided to come back home?"

Where is home, Amma? AJ asks when he is twelve, caught between uncertain childhood and angry adulthood. *I don't belong in New Zealand. In Sri Lanka, I'm less than a dog. So where exactly is home?*

The boy becomes a man who leaves in 2003 to fight a war he thinks is his. She is angry when he leaves, so she does not cry. And now he is

surely captured, tortured, murdered; blown to smithereens by a bomb.

"I know it *here*, Annie," Nisha says. She places her palm against her chest. Across vast oceans, across the schism of ideological differences, she knows. "The absence of AJ; it woke me a week ago." She doesn't mention the content of her dream: AJ's hands cupping her face, his eyes bloodshot, his lips mouthing *sorry*. She woke because she felt someone shake her shoulder. But no one was there, just Sam snoring.

Parents should not have to bury their children. *I will come to you,* she whispers. *I will gather you up like the scent of jasmine, the drunkenness of gold, the frantic whipping of a* kabaragoya's *tail.*

The burial ceremony does not bury her grief. It opens up a maw inside her, a wormhole of darkness that calls to her across water and land. She needs to see him. She has not been back since she left fifteen years ago, but she starts to pack the next day. She does not tell Sam. He'd scoff, then yell, perhaps hide her passport. *He does these things because he cares,* she tells herself. Sometimes love looks like fear.

Since January, the only news from Sri Lanka is death. The 2002 ceasefire, four years old, is crumbling.

FIVE TAMIL STUDENTS KILLED BY SPECIAL TASK FORCE AT TRINCO BEACH

GOMORANKADAWALA MASSACRE: 6 SINHALA RICE FARMERS GUNNED DOWN BY LTTE

SRI LANKAN NAVY KILL 13 TAMIL CIVILIANS IN ALLAIPIDDY IN RETALIATION FOR SAILOR DEATHS

ATTEMPTED ASSASSINATION OF GENERAL FONSEKA BY PREGNANT BLACK TIGER SUICIDE BOMBER: INTERNATIONAL CONDEMNATION

CLAYMORE MINE KILLS TROOPS IN JAFFNA

AJ is nine when Sam visits the tea plantation, high in the central hills of Kandy. Nisha knows white men often look at her with desire. She

wonders what they look like naked, the paleness of their flesh. Nisha in her mid-twenties, not yet broken by eleven-hour 500-rupee days. Proud eyes, leopard moving in the jungle of her flesh.

This white man, Sam: he is persistent. He comes back to the plantation day after day and asks for time alone with Nisha. The plantation owner senses a lucrative deal. Nisha is sure money changes hands. The white man says he's in love. She's the most "exotic" thing he's ever seen, he can't keep his hands off her. He offers her a ticket out. She takes it. New Zealand is a cold place with warm people, and she is grateful for her new life.

But AJ struggles. He refuses to listen to Sam. Hisses behind his back when he thinks Sam can't hear. *Fucking FAKE batshit.* Metal rod against bucking soul. *You're not my father!* Nisha hugs him tight and he protests, wriggles free.

He never finds out who his real father is, because Nisha never tells him. The Sinhala plantation owner's son, the quiet boy who fell in love with the Tamil tea-picker. So young, both of them. Stolen moments in her family's

shack. In the laundry of the big house. A dry patch of jungle floor. The sudden whisking away of the boy to study overseas as soon as Nisha's pregnancy becomes the number-one topic of gossip on the plantation; she never sees him again, and the pain of this calcifies into anger, hard as coconut shells in her heart. The union of lion and tiger produces a terrible hybrid, but a hybrid who is like his father: sensitive, nervy, a poet. How does such a soul become a terrorist? Or a freedom fighter – where does the truth of war lie? The irony of a half-Sinhalese man fighting other Sinhala men.

The calls from AJ are sporadic. A hesitant tingle of Nisha's ringtone, a vibration beside her ear, and she shoots out of bed to cradle the phone like a lover. Sometimes he calls from a public phone somewhere in Tiger-controlled Mannar district, or Kilinochchi township. Sometimes from deep within the jungle in Mullaitivu, staticky on a satellite phone. The last call was two weeks ago, and he'd sounded tired and frustrated.

I'm fine, Amma. Yes, I'm eating. Food, *Amma, that's what I'm eating! The leaders have big plans,*

I can't say much, but you'll hear on the news. Soon. I'll be home soon.

He's lying to make her feel better. She lets herself believe him. AJ left New Zealand in winter; it is now winter again, an August wild with her sadness. She squeezes her eyes shut, clenches her fists, refuses to cry.

Nisha picks up the old images encased inside glass frames and thinks back to when she was fifteen. "Take them, Nisha," the Sinhala boy tells her as they lie on the floor of the disused shed. She rolls onto her stomach and puts her face close to the pictures. "They belong to your family more than they do to mine." The images are a touchstone, talismans to guide her into the future. Somewhere in Europe, various white men refined and developed photographic processes while Nisha's ancestors sweated under the Equatorial sun. The first image: a daguerreotype, silver and chalk darkening with light. A white man in a pith helmet surveys his kingdom while a coterie of indentured labourers squat with their sacks of freshly picked tea. *Camellia sinensis:* the British solution to replace

failed coffee crops. The 1860s or thereabouts. One of the woman squatting is Nisha's great-great-grandmother, Vellamma. All the women have their heads covered, their eyes lowered. A few brown men stand around with turbans on their heads, sarongs around their waists. No one smiles. There's a child with his bags of tea. The British abolished slavery in 1834, but Vellamma and her co-workers, transported to the Lankan highlands from Tamil Nadu, worked long hours for little pay and lived in utter squalor. Yet Vellamma's expression burns with fire, and the sheer vitality of her spirit refuses to rest, even now.

Nothing changes. A century passes. Independence. A Sinhala government labels Nisha's people "temporary immigrants", despite 200 years of contributing to the goddamn economy. Citizenship – finally – in 2003, but second-class. *Go and live in your shacks built by the British,* the government tells them; *there is nothing wrong, do not complain about the cold, about your hacking cough from the sooty fires of your cooking, do not be so bold as to look your*

masters in the eye. The Sri Lankan Tamils in the north and east look down on Nisha's sort of Tamil people. Is AJ an acceptable Tiger because of his foreign passport? Vellamma tells Nisha that the afterlife is blessedly free of all this class and caste rubbish.

The second image, taken twenty years later. A tintype, not as shiny as the daguerreotype. A thin sheet of metal coated with enamel, spread with photographic emulsion. Nisha's great-grandmother Velu, named after the Tamil queen who fought the British and won, leans against a bank with eight other women. Their faces lit by sun, shadows under chins. Above them, tea bushes slant up hillsides. The women wear saris tied over one shoulder, metal bracelets on their arms, wooden beads around their necks. Their feet are bare. Velu is the only one who stares directly at the camera; she looks exhausted but defiant. Nisha feels Velu inside her, a spiteful avatar hellbent on revenge.

"I've got a work trip to Singapore, love."

The lie slips out smoothly. It's only a half-lie; Nisha will attend a work conference for a few

days. But her mind is focused on the journey beyond. She will hide behind her married name. No one – not the government forces, not the Tigers – would dare hurt a foreign citizen. She tucks Buddy, AJ's tattered teddy bear, inside some clothes. *You'll come with me, and together we'll bring AJ home, eh, Buddy?* The bear's placid brown eyes watch her gently. *I'll be damned if I leave my only child to rot in that godforsaken country.*

She could have been so many things. A goddess dances in her bones, goddess-heat melts her eyes like wax. Somewhere inside her is a country of full-throated birds, fantastical as peacocks, bridal veils of green and iridescent turquoise set with the eyes of the giant Argus. Fleet-footed deer, spotted and quick-tailed. Monkeys that swing from branch to branch with the lithe ease of wild things. The rumbling tread of elephant feet, toes splayed against red mud, eyes that never forget. The ancient hymns sung by earth upheld by mountains, unfettered by cement or fence line or asphalt. This is the country she wants to call home.

She is eight when she starts to work. She picks and picks and the bags are heavy. The men work on another section of the plantation, cutting back overgrowth with curved *kokaththa* knives. Her leaf-picking stick gets hung up inside her hut at night. There is a school she attends sometimes, but families need income from small hands more than they need educated minds. Leeches crawl up bare legs. Don't pull them off or their bite marks bleed and bleed, Amma says. Apply salt solution so the little suckers shrivel and fall. The mist. The way the white tendrils caress her skin and face like a lover. The Sinhalese supervisor, fond of his arrack. The fog, thick and obscurant the morning he creeps up and clamps his hand over her mouth. The man lean and wiry, fuelled with liquor. He treats her like property, a mahogany chair to bear his weight, an antique spoon to feed him *kitul* treacle.

Katunayake airport is bare white walls and cement floors. It's 1 AM when the plane lands. A crowd mills around outside the barbed-wire barricade. Defence-force personnel are everywhere, khaki fatigues, polished boots,

Heckler & Koch automatic assault rifles in their hands. A porter grabs her backpack and heads toward a taxi. She doesn't need his help, but pays him a hundred rupees. She's packed light. Quick-dry trousers and shirts. A sturdy pair of shoes. There's no knowing how far she'll cover on foot. She plans to speak only English or threadbare Sinhalese; not a word of Tamil must spill from her lips, or someone might see who she really is. The streets of Colombo glow with golden orange lights. Fluorescent white tubes illuminate battered-metal shopfronts. GUNADASA JEWELLERS. NUWARA ELIYA ARRACK. CEYLON FERTILISERS. GREEN CABIN RESTAURANT, BAMBALAPITIYA. Nisha sinks inside her memories. A bullock cart kerbside. Ironwood trees, interspersed with frangipani. She winds the window down and the night air smells warm, dusty, the scent of frangipani luminous and citrusy; the Indian Ocean sighs nearby, and she catches black and silver glimpses of it as the taxi winds its way along the main Galle road, straight as a Dutch canal, arrowing south toward Galle Fort. Her Sinhalese is stilted and trips off her

tongue as she pays the driver and steps inside the Radisson Hotel.

The next morning she eats breakfast alone – fish curry and string hoppers and sambol – as she scans the papers. *The Daily News*, *The Island*, *Lankadeepa*. suicide bomber kills army deputy chief of staff kulatunga outside colombo. A mouthful of fish, rolled with string hopper. ltte attack bus to Anuradhapura, kill 64 civilians. A gulp of coffee, too sweet with condensed milk, makes her feel like a child again. kebithigollewa massacre: 140 dead in ne sri lanka. The sambol so fresh and so good she eats spoonfuls of it, and her lips swell with blood. tiger cadre requests asylum at us embassy, claims brainwashing. All the news in Colombo is carefully one-sided: there is no mention of any government-sanctioned killings.

Oily smoothness of coconut, freshly roasted spices, whole red chillies, sour tang of tamarind. The food more than just food: emotion and memories and fire, heat in her face, desire in her womb. AJ at eight: "This is the best food I've ever eaten, Amma." Everything starts and ends

with him. Every year, Nisha manages something special for AJ's birthday – fried fish from the lake, smuggled in by a helpful security guard in return for small sexual favours; mutton balls in exchange for one of her gold bracelets. For her only child she keeps her eyes low, her mouth shut, her legs wide, puts up with the long hours and the suffocating sweat of men she does not love. AJ stumbling into the hut. His mother on all fours, crying, her hair pulled back in the fist of a man, the supervisor behind her, thrusting. The supervisor throws a shoe at the boy and he stumbles out again.

Did AJ's anger start then? Or was he born angry, bathed in the amniotic fluid of a girl who wants too much?

She boards the 9.20 AM train to Kandy from Maradana Railway Station. After that, she'll take a bus to Kilinochchi. Contingent on the buses still running. She won't think about her fellow passengers, won't wonder if one of them is pretending to be pregnant while hiding a bomb on her belly. Things are heating up in the north and east. The papers talk of new curfews,

an impending state of emergency. If she gets stopped at a checkpoint, she's got her story down pat. *Visiting my sick sister. Yes sir, dying of cancer, sir. My last chance to see her, please officer, you don't want to be responsible for the grief of a foreigner. Do you?*

The prickly presence from the burial ceremony travels with her on the plane, sits with her during her conference in Singapore, boards the flight to Colombo with her. It now sits on an empty train seat and doesn't speak. Nisha both knows and doesn't want to know what it is. She knows it is not Vellamma or Velu. Both those women enter rooms with fanfare – objects drop to floors and splinter, ceiling fans whir so fast they almost sever themselves from their stems, the temperature fluctuates: hot, then bone-chill cold. Those old women know how to party, now that they are dead. "We're making up for the long hours we worked while alive," they always tell her, "you won't believe how much gold we can wear here, it's unbelievable." But this other presence is quiet and nervy and waiting for the chance to speak.

The tea plantation is unchanged. *Camellia. Sinensis.* Semen. Tears. The supervisor, long dead of alcoholic cirrhosis. She hears that he drowned in his own blood, rupturing swollen varices, gut surging into lungs. The spot on the riverbank where she and the Sinhalese boy first made love. Both of them the same age, but Nisha felt ashamed at being so experienced. The boy just a boy, and she loves him for it; his eyes wide with wonder, his fumbling fingers, incense smell of his hair from *pooja*. Her heart swells with memories of him, with a longing she's never felt for Sam. The old mansion with a new cream coat. Rusty iron replaced with shiny corrugated tin, shingles cleared of moss. The owners moving around inside – is he in there, does he have a respectable Sinhala wife and beautiful Sinhala children now? No one recognises her. Her hat wide, brim hiding face in shadow. As the tourist group walks through the plantation, she spots Kala and Parvati and Kuntha, the girls she once picked tea with: skins burnt by constant sun, backs curved question marks, faces *crêpe de chine*-d with lines. Nisha turns and stares at a

distant blue hill. The guide asks if she is from Japan, and the question catches her off guard. The silver-tip tea tastes bitter and metallic.

A text from Sam: *How's Singapore? Need a pick-up from the airport?*

I'll get a taxi. Sleep tight, love.

The bus to Jaffna. The A9 highway, open to traffic for now. In all her life, Nisha has never been north of Kandy. Dusty fields, thin-ribbed cattle, jumbles of barbed wire at army checkpoints. Do the soldiers look like teenagers because she is getting old? The bus stops often. Nisha takes it all in, these places she's heard about but never seen. Dambulla, with tin signs pointing to the Sigiriya rock fortress and ancient cave temples. The turn-off to Anuradhapura, with its 2,500-year-old ruins. Mihintale, a mountain peak the birthplace of Buddhism on the island, now a site of pilgrimage. Barbed wire and sandbags sprout everywhere like menacing mushrooms. The air full of ozone, crackly with electricity. An ocean of water pours from above: the mid-year monsoon. Cords of rain like thick silver ropes strike the dusty earth and turn the

soil slick with mud. The rain whips the ghosts of Vellamma and Velu, who are riding the coat-tails of the bus, whooping and cackling like crows. *I come from agitators, disruptors, warriors. I am leopard woman, I will fight for the body of my child.*

"National Identity Card, Madam!" The bus is about to enter Vavuniya, and Tiger-controlled territory. Everyone disembarks and waits for a new bus. A female soldier with broad shoulders checks papers. In her flatlining lips Nisha senses pain; burning anger crouches on the young woman's shoulders and tightens her neck, black as a storm cloud. A Bushmaster M4 assault carbine hangs on her right shoulder. Nisha is tired, her mind so dense with memories it moves like rubber sap. She pulls out her passport and the soldier eyes her suspiciously, but flicks through the pages, then throws the passport back at her. Disappointed. She'll need someone else to bully today.

The prickly presence speaks to her the night before: *Go to Kilinochchi. One kilometre out of town, on the road to Jaffna, you will see a dirt*

road into the jungle. Take it. You will walk for twenty hours. You will find a boy called Siva. You will know him when you see him – slit-soul cautious, yellow eyes like cobra; trust him with all your heart. Speak my name. He will take you to me.

Tiger cadres at LTTE checkpoints. Teenagers with acne and bloodshot eyes. It makes Nisha feel old in her bones, even though she is only forty-two. A teen mother herself once, an escapee from slavery. Old men stare at her breasts. A young man with a *tilak* of turmeric and ash on his forehead sits next to her and presses his thigh into hers, moves his hand toward his groin and smiles. The ghost of Vellamma sizzles with indignation, spits in his face. The man flinches in surprise and looks around, wondering at the sudden wetness. Nisha uses the distraction to shove his shoulder hard. She gets up and stands in the aisle. The bus driver stops the bus and gets off to pray at a Hindu *kovil* by the side of the A9 highway – cement walls painted in stripes of yellow and cream, thatched roof strung with red prayer flags, crouched under a spreading banyan

tree – before getting back on and continuing the journey north.

In the end that is all any of us ever have, Nisha thinks; prayers, which are just another word for stories, memories, familiar ghosts that reverberate down the centuries.

"LTTE Identity card!" the cadre barks, and leans toward her. His eyes glazed red, maybe on something chemical to stop him sleeping. Her New Zealand passport, the confused look on the young man's face, the disappointment as he gives her precious document back to her. Power is a drug; the more you get, the more you want. She hears him shouting at someone else further down the bus. She gets off at Kilinochchi and walks. Dusty streets. The monsoon rains dried up, the sun in full force, wetness in the air promising more rain soon. Even thinner cattle. Some children play marbles outside the Nallurbhavan Vegetarian Restaurant. An old woman squats by the roadside, sells drinks stacked inside a styrofoam box with Coca-Cola logos plastered on it. Nisha drinks a lukewarm Fanta in one gulp. She buys several packets of

murukku, seven fried lentil *vadai*, three packets of garlic chilli potato crisps and a two-litre bottle of water from the Aathuri Multi Shop. Armed Tigers on a camouflaged utility truck drive down the street. Everyone keeps out of their way.

How long is your conference? You left so suddenly, Nish. The neighbours say hi. Did you get to the Raffles Hotel? Those Singapore Slings. Yum.

When AJ leaves in the winter of 2003, he leaves suddenly. There one day, gone overnight, his teddy bear Buddy on his pillow with an apologetic look on his face. Nisha does not get the chance for a hug. AJ hates displays of emotion. She wants to tell him that old men start wars in which young men die. Nothing ever changes; the cycle of history repeats across aeons.

Can you reply to my texts, Nisha? This is bloody ridiculous!

She turns the phone off. Soon she will have no reception, anyway. An explosion booms in the south, back toward Kandy. Shockwaves ripple

through the air. Nisha imagines she hears the wailing of mothers. Everyone stops to listen. The Tiger truck speeds up and disappears around a corner. She walks and does not look back. Twenty minutes out of town she follows the dirt track into the jungle. *One foot in front of the other. Keep walking, don't look back.* She falls into rhythm with the prickly presence, which goose-steps beside her. Vellamma and Velu float through the trees ahead, uncharacteristically subdued. They look at her from time to time, then look away before she catches their eyes. If they know what is ahead, they aren't saying. The heat hypnotic, the lacey pattern of leaves on the ground like fretwork from an ancient civilisation. Right foot, left foot. A blister on her left foot starts to agitate. Termite mounds as high as her chin. Crows with strong black beaks, shoulders hunched and eyes hooded. A pile of bodies inside an open pit, hands tied behind their backs, fly-buzz stench so strong she almost vomits. Trance-state, dream-state. The alcoholic supervisor swaggers up to her holding his shrivelled penis in one hand, teeth loose in

rotting gums, tries to say something about his dreadful childhood. She hits him so hard he deflates like a punctured balloon. She is a child-woman, loose black hair billowing like raven feathers to her shoulders.

Five hours pass, then six, ten. She eats as she walks. Drinks as she walks. Descends into the underworld along a forest path flat and well-worn by combat boots. The sound of voices behind her, and she hides in a copse until the Tiger cadres pass by – the war is heating up, something big is happening, their excited chatter ricochets around the trees. Right foot, left foot. She has no more sweat, no more urine left in her body. Everything is dissolving, leaving behind just the essence. She is fire. Buddy sticks his head out of her backpack and whispers gently, "You know you'll stay with him, yes? You can't take him back, it's too dangerous. Home is here."

Twelve, fifteen, eighteen hours. She walks all night. She must find the only person she's ever loved. Rain falls, dust runs off her in rivulets of brown. She sticks her tongue out and it is reptilian with dryness. Twenty hours of walking,

her body so thin yet so heavy, reaches a clearing in the forest. A cobra's yellow eyes glint from deep inside a pile of sandbags. She speaks AJ's name, and the slither of cobra scales through a smaller path and further on, further in to a country she's always known she would find.

Selected Titles from Paper + Ink

www.paperand.ink

from Leeds University. She was a Jerwood/Arvon mentee in 2015–16, a Bridge Awards Emerging Writer in 2017, a second-place winner of the 2019 Yeovil Literary Prize and a longlistee for the 2021 Discoveries Prize, awarded by the Women's Prize. She has published stories in *Ambit, Mslexia, Fairlight Shorts, Litro, Honest Ulsterman, MIR* and *The First Line*. Her debut novel, *Dwell*, is currently on submission.

Himali McInnes
REGIONAL WINNER: THE PACIFIC

Himali McInnes works as a family doctor at a busy practice in Auckland, New Zealand, and in the prison system. She is a constant gardener, a chicken farmer and a beekeeper. She writes short stories, essays, flash fiction and poetry, and has been published in various journals and anthologies. Her book *The Unexpected Patient: True Kiwi Stories of Life, Death and Unforgettable Clinical Cases* was published in 2021 by HarperCollins.

Ocoee & Other Stories

WINNERS OF THE COMMONWEALTH SHORT STORY PRIZE 2023